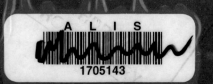

Fig was scared of a thousand things.

Scared of the dark and of getting lost, scared of spiders and other long-legged shadows.

She was afraid of questions, in case she did not know the answers, afraid of forgetting all the things she had already learned, frightened of the big, blustering boys at school.

Fig was even afraid of the silly sheep who shoved and shouldered past her in the pasture.

She was scared of the never-ending war, and her dreams swarmed with Belfuscans armed to their eggy teeth.

She hated the size of the seething sea and the weight of sky above it.

Once, everything frightened Fig.

Then Gulliver came.

For Oliver James. G.McC.

For Alex, my very own Fig, and for David Silver
who always loved tall stories. J.

OXFORD
UNIVERSITY PRESS
Great Clarendon Street, Oxford OX2 6DP

Oxford University Press is a department of the University of Oxford. It furthers the University's
objective of excellence in research, scholarship, and education by publishing worldwide in

Oxford New York
Auckland Cape Town Dar es Salaam Hong Kong Karachi Kuala Lumpur Madrid
Melbourne Mexico City Nairobi New Delhi Shanghai Taipei Toronto

With offices in
Argentina Austria Brazil Chile Czech Republic France Greece Guatemala Hungary
Italy Japan Poland Portugal Singapore South Korea Switzerland Thailand Turkey Ukraine Vietnam

Oxford is a registered trade mark of Oxford University Press in the UK and in certain other countries

Text copyright © Geraldine McCaughrean 2005
Illustrations copyright © Jago 2005

First published 2005

British Library Cataloguing in Publication Data available

ISBN-13: 978 0 19 279130 6
ISBN-10: 0 19 279130 3

10 9 8 7 6 5 4 3 2 1

Printed in Thailand.

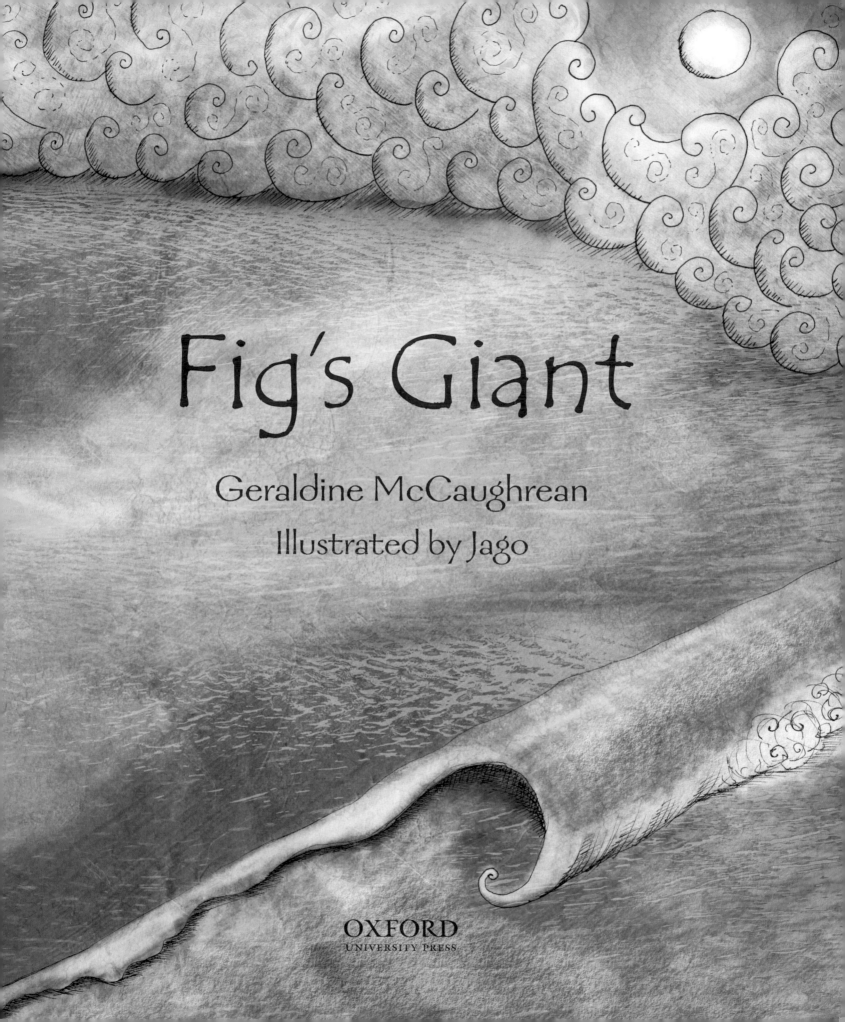

Fig's Giant

Geraldine McCaughrean

Illustrated by Jago

OXFORD
UNIVERSITY PRESS

The summer storm scared Fig terribly. Its thunder crashed against Lilliput like cannonfire, and the lightning seemed to be peeling the ceiling off her bedroom. All night she could hear the sea hunting for ships to swallow.

So she was glad when, by morning, the storm had died away, and she could go out to play with Tolgo on the beach.

The sand was strewn with wreckage – huge beams of splintered wood.

That was when she saw them – two sand-brown towers
standing on the beach, their tops rounded like gravestones.
   'More wreckage,' thought Fig at first.
   But Tolgo whimpered and hung back. Fig ran to get a better view.
   'It's a whale,' she whispered.
   But whales don't wear shirts and trousers and shoes.
   Whales don't have hands as big as sheep-pens or faces
stubbly with beard.

'It's a – a...' But words would
not come big enough to describe
the monster on the beach.
'It's a – MAN!' breathed Fig.
And Tolgo had to agree.

'He's dead,' said Fig.

She crept right up close, heart thumping. 'Definitely dead.'

She climbed the ladder of chilly fingers, then out along the arm, until she reached the chest.

'Come on up, Tolgo,' she said. 'It's perfectly safe.'

Then she was jumping up and down, shouting at the seagulls:

'Look at me! I'm the king of the castle.

Get down you dirty rascals!

I'm the king of the Big! I'm Fearless Fig!

I —'

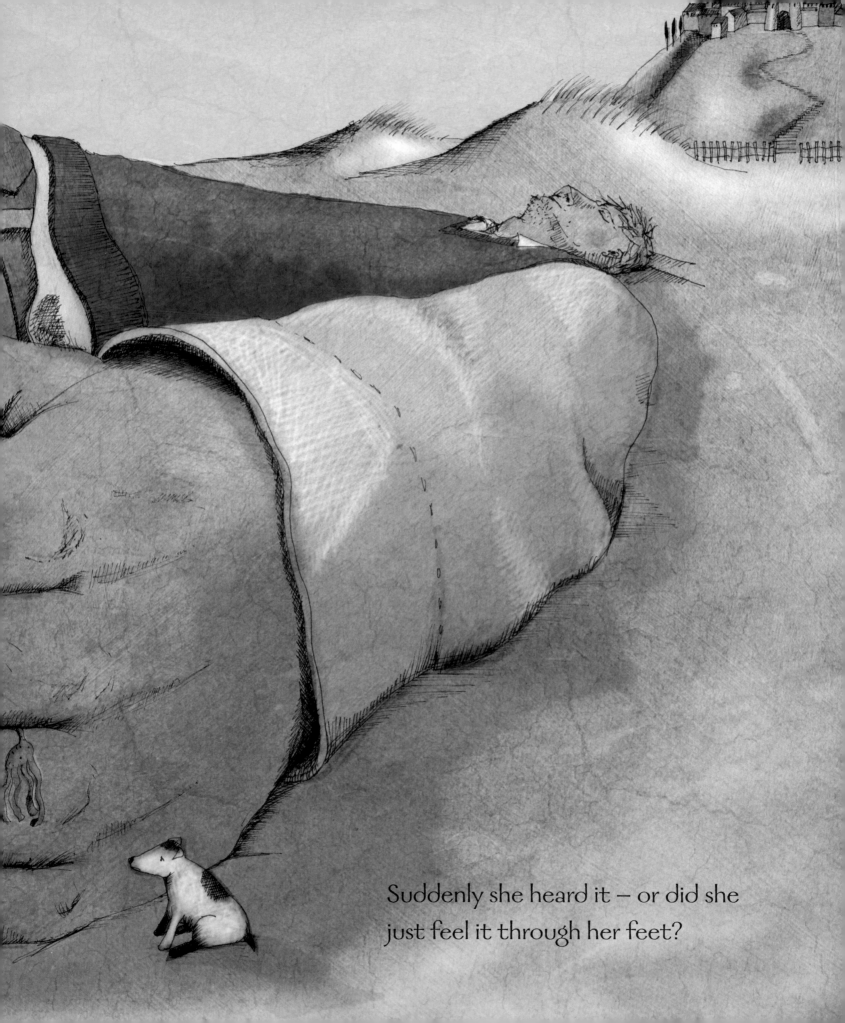

Suddenly she heard it – or did she
just feel it through her feet?

The blue woollen ground under her quaked with the giant's heartbeat:

BANG BANG BANG

. . . and the giant head rolled sideways.

He wasn't dead at all!

The dog jumped one way. Fig jumped the other.

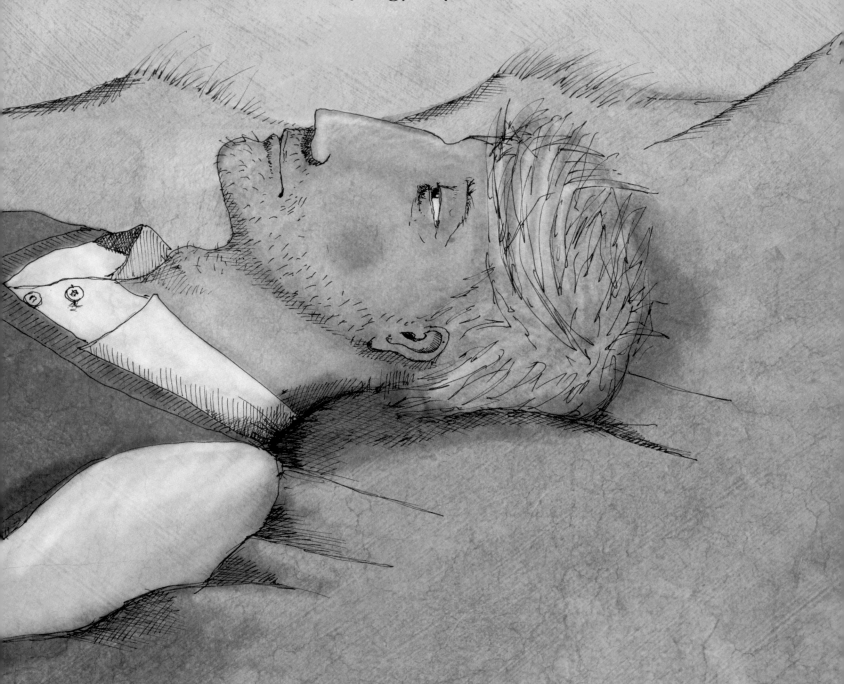

Boots full of sand, mouth empty
of spit, she picked up her heels and
RAN, every moment expecting giant
fingers to pluck her up and a giant
mouth to swallow her down.

She ran and ran until she reached the city walls. No breath to shout, no voice to call, Fig leaned against the city gateway, panting and winded.

'On the beach! Come quick! There's a . . . a giant! There's a giant on the beach! Come quick!'

But no one would believe her.

From house to house she ran, beating on the doors. She rattled at the gates in front of the royal palace.

'There's a giant on the beach! Come quick!'

But nobody would come.

So she climbed to the top of the temple tower and rang the bell.

CLANG
CLANG
CLANG

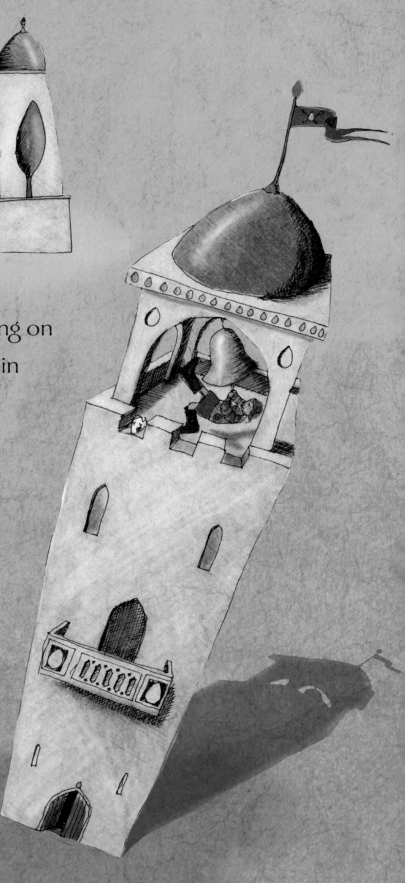

The whole army turned out then —
foot soldiers and archers and cavalry.

'What? Are the Belfuscans invading?
Have the Belfuscans landed?'
Running and galloping and kicking
up the sand in clouds, the whole army
pelted down to the sea, thinking they
were under attack.
Fig ran, too.

When they saw the giant, some turned and
ran away again. The rest froze with fright.

'Shshsh! Don't wake him!'
said Fig to the captain.

'Shshsh!'
said the captain
to his troops.

'Kaaaawk!'
said the seagulls.

'Shshsh!'
said the soldiers
to the seagulls.

But still Fig's giant
did not stir.

He did not stir even while they lashed him down with rope.
At last, when he was netted like summer strawberries, they began
to be brave again, swaggering about and sticking out their tongues.
  'That's put him in his place!' declared the captain.
  At last, the giant opened his eyes and found he could not move.
  'Poor giant,' thought Fig sadly. 'I should have kept you a secret.'
  Then:

TWANG TWANG
TWANG

The giant was breaking free!
'*Shoot!*' yelled the captain. '*Shoot!*'

'*Ouch!*' said the giant, as arrows
pricked his hands and body.
'Poor giant,' thought Fig. 'I'm sorry.'

'It looks hungry,' said the captain. 'Better feed it, in case it has a mind to eat us.' So everyone ran to fetch food.

And how the giant ate! Whole roasted sheep! Whole spits of chickens! Three loaves at a time!

Fig was just balancing another basket of loaves on her head when she saw the captain pour a bag of powder into a barrel of wine.

'Now, men,' he said. 'Take him this to drink. That should do the trick!'

'*Don't drink! It's poisoned!*' shouted Fig.

She ran to the giant's hand and smacked it as hard as she could.

She jumped into his cuff and, as he reached

for the barrel, clung on for a dizzying ride.

    'Don't drink, giant!'

    But her giant was a foreigner. He did not

understand the language of Lilliput.

He swigged down

the wine . . .

GLUG
GLUG
GLUG

. . . and fell into a

deep, deep sleep.

Not poisoned,

after all, but drugged.

So that is how Fig Fogle came to ride a giant all the way back
to the city. The army built a wooden platform on wheels,
and winched him aboard for the journey inland. Kneeling
on his chest, Fig thought, 'You are my giant. I found you.
I'll look after you.'

   He had to have somewhere to live. You can't
just leave a man out in the rain and
wind – even if he is as big as a tree.
So the emperor gave him, for a
prison, the huge ruined temple
on the hill outside town.

Fig's giant did not argue. He crawled in and out through the
little door of his draughty prison like a dog kept in a kennel.
Fig went up there every day to talk to him.
In time, the giant began to understand
what she said, and even to speak
a few words of Lilliputian.
He said his name was Gulliver.
Lemuel Gulliver.

People came to stare and point at Gulliver, to gasp and gawp and gape. They would sketch him and measure him and paste adverts on his back. They would sniff him, climb him, and shelter from the rain under his knees. They even plucked strands of his hair for fishing lines.

But Fig simply went there to play. Gulliver was her friend.

He could throw a ball for Tolgo which took ten minutes to fetch.

He even let Fig play in his pockets.

What marvellous things there were in there! There was a comb as big as a fence, and a pair of round windows joined together with wire. There were gold coins as big as cartwheels, and a sheet big enough for the emperor's bed.

But most marvellous of all was a round gold chest full of cogs and pivots and springs, all whirring and whirling about, like a huge mechanical heart:

TICK

TICK

TICK

Gulliver told Fig how he had been shipwrecked by the storm, and how, in his country, everyone was as big as he was. 'I wouldn't hurt you, little Fig, nor any of your countrymen,' he said. 'Not for the world.'

That is why Fig screwed up all her courage, went to the palace door, and knocked at the big gate:

BLAM

BLAM

BLAM

'Please set Gulliver free,' she said to the emperor.
'My giant's a good giant. I give you my word on it.'

Next day, the emperor himself went to visit Gulliver.

'One thing I must know, before we free you, giant! At which end do you open a boiled egg?'

Gulliver turned to Fig and asked, 'Is he joking or is he mad?'

So Fig had to explain about the war.

'For many years, we Lilliputians have been at war with the Belfuscans across the sea, because they open their boiled eggs at the Big End, when everyone knows you open eggs at the Pointy End.'

Gulliver listened carefully.

Then he threw back his head and laughed.

'HOO HOO! HOO!'

The emperor was puzzled. War was a serious business, after all.

Gulliver slapped his knees and rocked to and fro, hooting. 'Pointy End, indeed.'

The emperor smiled warmly and ordered the chains to be taken off at once. 'Good answer, sir! I am glad to hear you are a right-thinking man, sir, and a friend to Lilliput!' he said.

Next day, Fig was doing arithmetic when the teacher screamed and dropped a pile of books. A face as big as a planet was bulging in at the window.

'Oh, don't worry. That's just my friend Gulliver,' said Fig.

The big, bad, blustering boys stared, round-eyed and open-mouthed.

'Good morning, Figgy,' said Gulliver. 'I've been talking to the emperor about eggs, and I've hatched a kind of plan. Care to come for a trip?'

'Thank you. I'd be delighted,' Fig replied.

'Where are we going?' she asked as she and Tolgo rode along on Gulliver's shoulder.

'To Belfuscu. To stop this ridiculous war.'

Suddenly Fig was not delighted, not delighted at all.
But there was no getting down, no going back.
Gulliver strode down to the beach and waded into the sea . . .

DEEPER AND DEEPER . . .

until Fig thought they would both drown for sure!
But for Gulliver, even the deepest deeps of
Lilliput Channel came only up to his chin.

Ahead lay the coastline of Belfuscu – a harbour crowded with soldiers and sailors and three-masted men-o'-war.

Like a sea monster Gulliver rose from the waves. Then on he went wading, wading ashore.

Somewhere on land an alarm bell began to ring.

Within the harbour walls, Gulliver calmly gathered ropes into the palm of his giant hand.

The startled Belfuscan troops shook themselves and raised their bows; arrows swarmed into the sky.

But Gulliver had already turned his back, and was wading out again, across the harbour, his body frosted with silver, bristling arrows. And behind him – like party balloons on the end of their strings – bobbed the whole Belfuscan fleet.

Heroes they came home, Fig and her giant.
Their names were sung in songs and written down
in history books.

Everyone danced in the streets, because the Great Boiled Egg
War had been won.

'Tomorrow you shall go back, and make the Belfuscans
our slaves!' declared the emperor.

'No,' said Gulliver. 'I won't do that. All men should be free
of war and free of slavery. I'm sorry, but no.'

The emperor turned very pale.
The dancing stopped.
The people scattered.

The emperor and his ministers of state
met in secret to whisper and plan.

'Won't make slaves
of our enemies?'

'Who does he
think he is?'

'Won't obey
the emperor?'

'Won't go back
to Belfuscu?'

'The man is
plainly a villain!'

'The man is
talking treason!'

'Won't do what
we want?'

'Gulliver! Lemuel Gulliver, wake up!'

Fig heaved open the heavy temple doors.

'The bishop says you are a spy. The prime minister says you are a rebel! The emperor says you are a traitor! I heard them whispering nose-to-nose!

Gulliver sat up so quickly that he banged his head.

'They decided not to shoot you with poisoned arrows . . .'

'Good,' said Gulliver, pulling on his shoes.

'They decided not to burn down the temple with you asleep inside . . .'

'How kind!' said Gulliver.

'They decided not to send the army to fight you . . .'

'I should hope not!' said Gulliver, fastening his trousers.

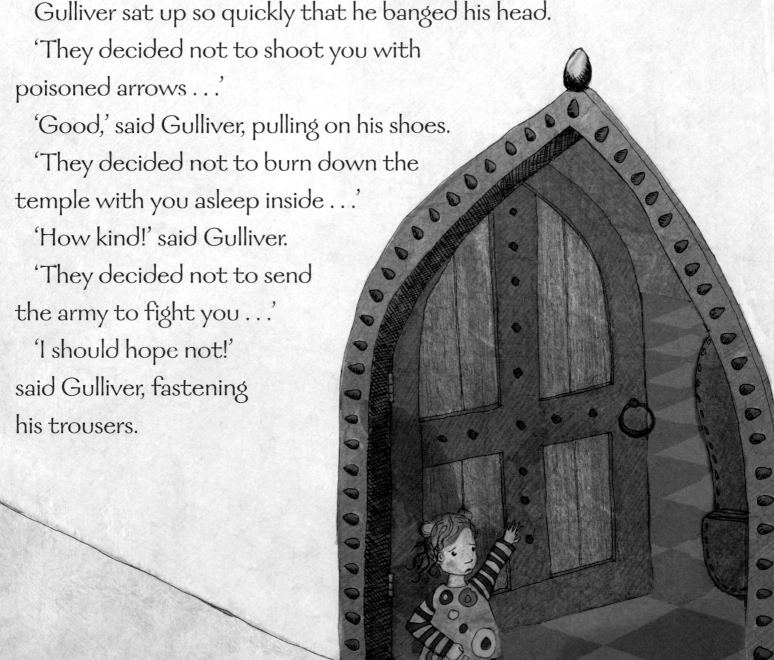

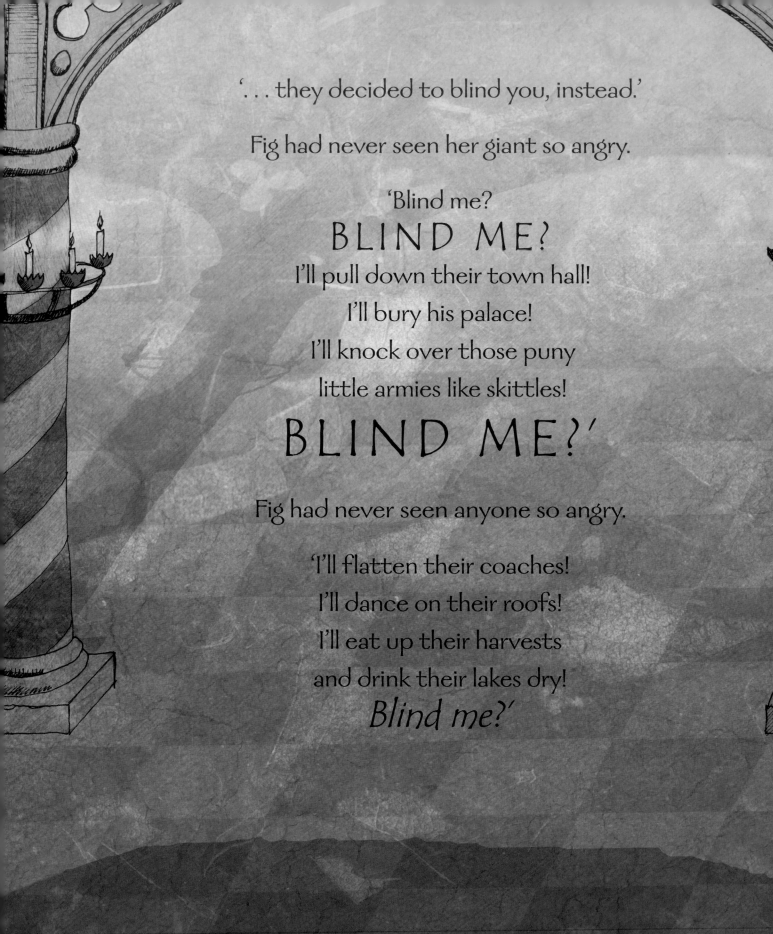

'. . . they decided to blind you, instead.'

Fig had never seen her giant so angry.

'Blind me?
BLIND ME?
I'll pull down their town hall!
I'll bury his palace!
I'll knock over those puny
little armies like skittles!
BLIND ME?'

Fig had never seen anyone so angry.

'I'll flatten their coaches!
I'll dance on their roofs!
I'll eat up their harvests
and drink their lakes dry!
Blind me?'

Then Gulliver looked down at Fig.
'Please don't,' she said.
'Of course I won't,' he said.
'Here, dry your eyes on my handkerchief.'
The white sheet smothered Fig from head to foot.
'But I'm not staying here to be blinded!
There is far too much in the world I want to see!'

So Gulliver rolled his clothes together in a bundle and walked down to the sea once more.

On the way, he scooped up a handful of sheep and put them in his pockets, like humbugs.

Choosing the biggest galleon in the harbour, he put out to sea, though the ship was scarcely bigger than a bath for him.

Over the horizon he floated — one tiny giant on the endless, restless sea. And there he was spotted by a ship from his own quarter of the world.

Back in England, he let the little Lilliputian sheep loose to graze in a public park, where the giants and giantesses crowded to see them, though they did not much believe how he had come by them.

Until Fig told them, too.

Well, who else do you think he would have trusted to be his shepherd? Who else had a sheepdog the right size? Who else would have kept him company on the long voyage home?

Who else would he want to wear, like a feather in his cap, come what may and come what might?

When he sets sail tomorrow, on a new adventure, Fig and Tolgo will go with him then, too.

After all, what is there to be afraid of, when you have a friend?